Udehori

腕雕

Isshin Mei

一心命

THE TATTOOED ARM
A STORY OF DEDICATION

Written by Shikitei Sanba 式亭三馬
Illustrated by Utagawa Kunimitsu 歌川国満
Translated by Eric Shahan シャハン・エリック

Translator's Introduction

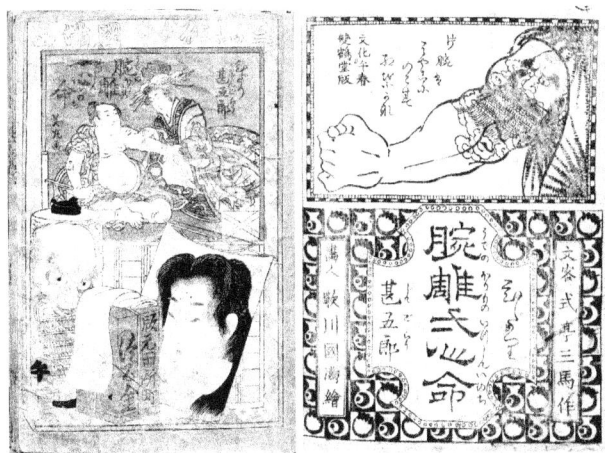

This is the first in a series to reproduce and translate classic Japanese manga (comic books/cartoons) of the early modern era.

The Tatooed Arm

The Tattooed Arm was published in 1810 and was written by Shikitei Sanba and illustrated by Utagawa Kunimitsu who produced and illustrated many similar Manga. The style of manga very popular in Edo are generally referred to as *Kusazōshi,* but their content evolved over time.

Origins of *Kusazōshi* (Leaves of Grass Books)

In the early 1600s the tumultuous Warring States Period ended. These near endless wars had raged since 1467 were finally resolved to establish the beginnings of the peaceful Edo Era. Freed from constant war, average citizens became able to work and trade freely within the bounds of the feudal system. Literacy rates began to rise as the emerging merchant class sent their children to temple schools and private tutors. With a higher rate of literacy a market in mass produced books and pamphlets emerged, and in the 1660s a new kind of book emerged called *Kusazōshi* 草双紙 ("grass leaves books.") The early *Kusazōshi* were adventure tales first geared towards women and children, who had become literate due to the temple schools, however they soon became popular with a wider range of people. This resulted in more sophisticated stories with elaborate art and layouts, eventually becoming sarcastic critiques of modern society. The genre survived until the beginning of the Meiji Era in 1868 and the advent of modern printing presses to Japan.

Evolution

Both the style and content of *Kusazōshi* changed over time and researchers have categorized them by the color of the outer cover which changed as the style evolved. The covers of the books went from red, black, blue and finally yellow. At each stage the stories became more complex and expanded in length as the art became more sophisticated and the stories more complex. The earliest *Kusazōshi,* red covered books, were single stories while later yellow-cover books could be up to ten parts, split into 20 books. Each part of the story would be sold separately. Later, the multiple parts of the book would be bound into single volume. This is similar to how modern Japanese manga are sold first a chapter at a time in weekly magazines and then later compiled into a book.

The illustration above by Settan Hasegawa (1778–1843)長谷川雪旦 shows the *Lucky Crane House Uemon* 鶴屋喜右衛門

4

bookshop in Edo. This is a Local Book Shop 地本問屋 that sold illustrated *Kusazōshi* as well as Ukiyo-e Floating World prints of heroes, actors and landscapes.

Earlier books were unattributed while later books attributed both the names of the writer and artist. Also the original adventure stories and simple fairy tales gave way to abbreviated versions of Kabuki plays and classic stories. Eventually the Kibyōshi 黄表紙 (yellow cover) books published before 1791, began satirically to reference contemporary figures and contemporary Japanese society. However, in 1791, strict censorship laws ended political satire and publications were prohibited from discussing current events and politics. Government censors decreed all printed matter had to be reviewed and approved before publication; approved publications carried a detailed notice of the censors' approval. Sanctions against publishing unapproved material were draconian, which caused the writers and artists to switch to tales of morality or stories of revenge.

How were they made?

Each book is usually five woodblock prints sewn together. One story typically consists of three books for a total of 15 pages, though some are longer or shorter. The Hiragana Japanese phonetic syllabary was used with few Kanji, making them very readable.

Who read them?

The Samurai class, about 7% of the population, was literate; however, starting in the 17th century the expanding merchant class also began to educate their children. In Edo, today's Tokyo and the home base of the ruling Tokugawa *Bakufu* military government, the literacy rate was estimated to have been around 80% for males and 25 % for females, compared with the national average of 40-50% overall. *Kusazōshi* as a form of popular literature, were targeted mainly to women and children; however, they were undoubtedly read by Samurai (albeit perhaps covertly.)

Are they hard to translate?

Japanese is already one of the more difficult languages to learn, in fact, according to the US State Department's Foreign Service Institute, modern Japanese is the most difficult language for a native

English speaker to acquire basic fluency. Edo Era (1603-1868) Japanese is even more difficult, written in archaic style heavily influenced by ancient written Chinese and these books include witty and ironic commentary on contemporary society. The original script is a special type of handwritten, cursive Japanese that is illegible even to most educated Japanese today. Despite years of practice I often cannot fully read the original text in most *Kusazōshi*; however, transcriptions of the text into standard Japanese letters are available. Though these books help in reading the text, the language and humor is still very much from the 17th~19th century Japan.

Even the arrangement of text and illustrations on one page is a bit of an adventure in itself, as it is not always clear who is saying what, when and in what order. In a sense it doesn't matter and I suspect that contemporary readers likely enjoyed piecing the story of each scene together. Below is a general diagram of how the text proceeds.

Back cover image: Cover of *The Tattooed Arm.*

腕雕一心命 *The Tattooed Arm: A Story of Dedication* 1810
By Shikitei Sanba 式亭三馬
Illustrations by Utagawa Kunimitsu 歌川国満

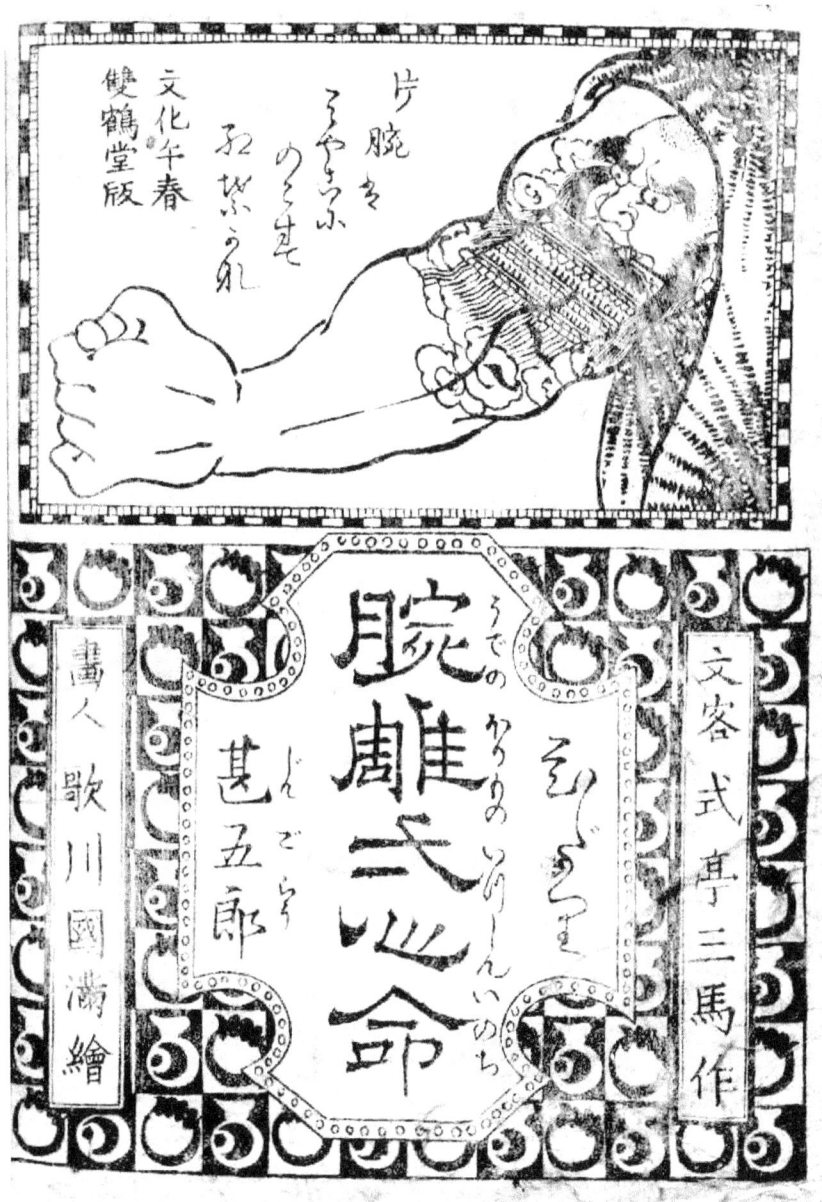

Title page of *The Tattooed Arm*

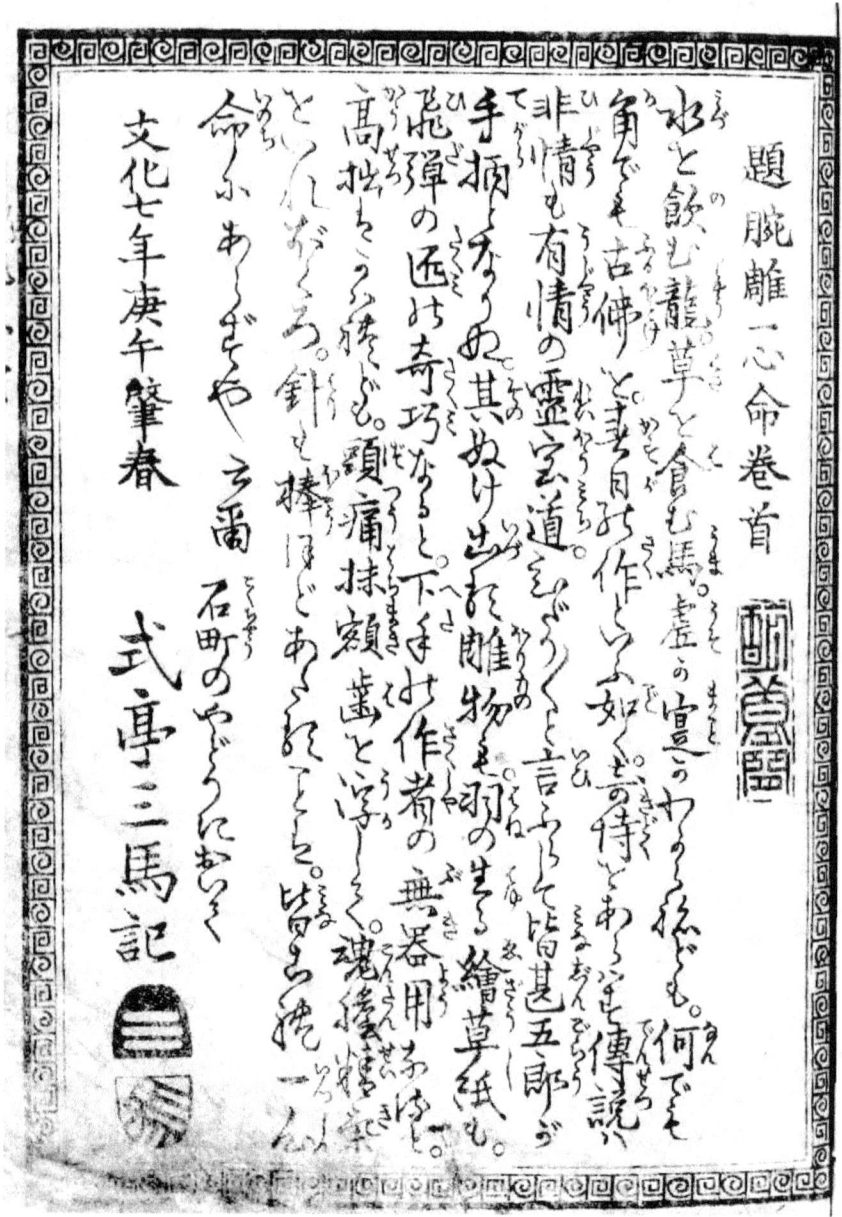

腕雕一心命 *The Tattooed Arm: A Story of Dedication*
Introduction
Shikitei Sanba
Spring of 1810

As you all know long, long ago there was an artist by the name of Kose no Kanaoka 巨勢金岡. He was a Japanese master of Chinese painting (who lived in the 9th century.) There was also the engraver Hidari Jingoro 左甚五郎, known as "Lefty" (a semi-legendary engraver said to have been active in the early Edo Era 1596 – 1644.)

Both of these artists were legendary in their ability to create masterworks. Like a dragon that could call forth a cloud and rise to the heavens, or a horse wandering around at night munching on Japanese clover in front of the Emperor's Japanese clover room. (So named because it featured pictures of Japanese clover painted on it to match a real clover outside.) Therefore there were a multitude of great and mysterious things associated with their works. However, we will not dwell on all of those rather, I encourage you to feast your eyes on the topic.

This tells the story of the master illustrator and five self-styled gentlemen heroes from Osaka. The first is Hoeti Ichiuemon, but he is a bit of a coward so he only plays a bit role. The next is Kari "Goose" Kanabunshichi, Gokui Senuemon "Seal (as in name seal/chop)", An-no Hirahyoei "Safety" and Kaminari Atsugoro "Thunder."

The four were determined to make it big and poured their efforts into one project or another. The four men discussed their situation. One declared: *You know we aren't going to get*

anywhere if we don't all have Horimono (literally an engraving but in this case meaning tattoos.)

Another said: *But if we go to an amateur it will hardly add to our image. Hmm…I think we should get Master Kose to do the drawing and then get Master Lefty to do the engraving. What say ye all?*

The other men all replied, *A splendid plan indeed!*

They spent the rest of the night drinking and refining their plan. The next day they all stomped over to Kose's house and inquired of the two artisans,

Kose Sensei, Lefty Sensei we don't really care what you do, just make it spectacular! If the tattoos aren't created by you they will lack majesty!

Kose and Lefty were stunned at the request to make art that would be engraved on the human body. Carving something into the body given to you by your mother and father seemed illogical, but they figured if they made a fuss the group would start trouble, so they set about their work. They silently began the process of drawing the illustrations and carving.

The four men were engraved with such total concentration that the tattoos seemed to be living reincarnations.

1. Goose got the scene of Watanabe fighting the demon Ibaraki at Rashomon gate tattooed on his back.

Note: Watanabe no Tsuna 渡邊綱 (953-1025) was a Samurai who served Minamoto no Yorimitsu. This story, which occurred in Kyoto, revolves around a demon by the name of Ibaraki Doji who haunted the Rashomon Gate harassing those that passed through. When Watanabe passed through, Ibaraki grabbed Watanabe, who in the ensuing struggle cuts Ibaraki's arm off.

2. Thunder got the image of Omori Hikoshichi 大森彦七being beset by the soul of the vanquished Kusunoki in the form of a female devil.

Note: The Samurai Omori defeated the forces of Kusunoki Masashige at the battle of Minato River in 1336, which lead to Kusunoki committing suicide. In this 1772 print by Katsukawa Shunsho, Omori, who is on his way to a spring festival in 1342, encounters a beautiful girl standing by the riverbank. He offers to carry her across and she climbs on his back. As he carries her across the river she grows heavier and heavier. Turning back he sees there is a demon on his back. Another version of the story states he notices her face reflected in the water and sees she has horns. Though Omori thinks he is helping a woman in distress, he suddenly realizes she is a devil. This scene can be found in many prints, figurines and even Tsuba sword guards.

3. Seal got a tattoo of Kagekiyo grabbing the Shikoro (neck guard-flap) on the back of Juro Mihonoya's helmet.

Note: A famous scene from a 12th century battle which can also be found on many prints, figurines and Tsuba sword guards. The illustration above is from a Meiji Era Kabuki play starring Ichikawa Danjuro as Kagekiyo and Ichikawa Sadanji as Mionoya. The scene was part of a battle in the Genpei War. It shows Fujiwara Kagekiyo 藤原景清 grabbing the Shikoro back flap of 美尾屋十郎 Mionoya Juro's helmet. The helmet ripped off before Kagekiyo could take his head. Though he got away, Kagekiyo famously raised Juro's helmet up with the butt of his halberd.

4. Safety got the severed head of the 17th century Samurai "Hog Bear" Inokuma Noritoshi 猪熊教利 on one arm and the head of the woman he was found having an adulterous affair with on the other arm.

Note: The story of the "Inokuma Affair" is a little confused, but basically involved an orgy amongst high ranking Samurai and wives of nobles, led by Inokuma, who was apparently very handsome. While they should have all been beheaded according to the customs of the day (and some stories claim they were), due to politics only lesser penalties were doled out. There is also a tale that Inokuma is a monk who was executed for adultery.

	**Dialogue from the previous pages** Lefty: *Getting a tattoo like that Chinese warrior called 9 Dragons is nothing compared to what you are asking for. It is going to require three colors, so it will hurt quite a bit.*
	Goose: *Pain doesn't hurt, do as you must!*
	Safety: *Oh, be quiet you fool, stop trying to look so calm!*
	Serving Woman: *Oh, Safety! Speak politely! Kiss, Kiss!*

Thunder:

That woman's head has a real obstinate look about her. Oh my, I think I recognize that face!

Kose:

Rather than talking about how stiff that woman's neck is, we should talk about how thick the fat on your back is! My ink is slipping and sliding all over the place. I once got so frustrated at losing a painting contest against a young lad I hurled my brush away in anger, but now I will have to destroy it because it is all greasy.

Seal:

Doesn't matter if Kose is throwing his brush out or his back out, seems like he's got a lot of animosity towards that brush....

These four men got the greatest tattoos in Japan, therefore they felt they were at the peak of their adventure. The men completely bonded with their tattoos. However, skillful works like these have mysterious powers. As they slept soundly that night, the four men's tattoos began to move and pull away from their hosts and flit and float about in the sky.

Later, the tattoos separated from the bodies of the four men, so floating in the air there was a devil, Samurai and the severed head of a man and a woman.   The floating tattoos called out to one another.

Ibariki the Demon :

Hmm, I think I might head to the shore of Rashomon. The arm I grabbed the helmet with is fine, but the one I was holding onto the pillar of the gate with is stiff! Oh, it is sore! I may need to get a massage...

Omori Hikonana : *I'm so sick of having that lady on my back like I'm some kind of new mother. I wouldn't mind heading to the shore sometime...say, where did that Devil Girl go? She's probably gossiping with the other ladies at the end of the barracks housing...and I'm getting a little peckish. Some soba noodles would be great, especially a double portion!*

Devil Girl :

It may look easy, haunting a person by climbing onto their back but, it is really is a serious business. Nothing at all like riding in a palanquin! My legs get all stiff!

Watanabe :

Well, while that demon is away I have some choices to make, like whether to hang out or hang out the laundry. Maybe I will pop over to Dojoji temple and buy a protective amulet for my back.

Woman's severed head :

Inukuma! Would you hurry up! Fly up over here!

Inukuma :

You know if we are seen in the daytime flying around like this people will think we are kites! By the way, that piece of paper you got in your mouth is nothing! I have this big heavy chunk of armor. Its liable to break my teeth! What terrible luck!

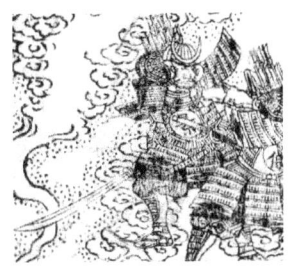

Kagekiyo :

Stop trying to shake me off, Mihonoya. I have to spend all my time staring at your back! It's boring! Hey, where are you going? Take me!

Mihonoya :

Alright already! Let go and I will let you tag along! Geez, what a pain in the ass!

The ghost of Kusunoki found a nice place in the shadows of a grove of willow trees. The ghost held her famous thin shawl over her head when the head of the circus appeared from behind a pile of lumber. The man went by the name Manbachi, a name composed of two Kanji, Man 万 meaning 10,000 and Bachi 八, meaning 8.

There is a famous Japanese saying, "Out of every 10,000 things only 8 are true." This suited Manbachi, who was a schemer. This evening Manbachi was planning to catch up with a girl he was friendly with by the name of Four Day Month Little Hundred, or Pandora (the name implies a person who causes more and more mischief.)

Manpachi had promised to meet Pandora on her way home and divert her to his abode for some fun. Seeing a female figure in the shadows he called out.

Hey! Pandora! You're late! Its nearly midnight. Don't play coy let's get moving!

He offered his hand to her but the Devil Girl with the cloak over her head did not react. Manpachi tried a little charm,

That is quite a mask you have there, between that and the Yukata you have over your head you are doing a great job keeping the mosquitos away.

The Devil Girl did not reply but extended both arms, startling Manpachi.

You want me to carry you on my back? A piggy back ride? You are awfully demanding today...are we suddenly like the 14 year old O-tomo and the 38 year old Nagauemon trying to elope before being killed like in the Kabuki play?

Devil Girl:

Thanks for carrying me, your back is a nice change from the other guy.

Omori Hideshichi had a free space on his back for a person but the Devil Girl was nowhere to be found. Despite the fact that she was the ghost of Kusanoki, they had formed a kind of bond. The relationship was not as bad as one would have you believe, in fact it was like they were married. Omori kept rubbing his back where he usually carried the girl.

He kept looking until he spied the what he thought was the Devil Girl underneath a willow tree.

Hey, what are you doing? Stop fooling around! You were so late I had to go searching for you! Come on, hop to it! Get on my back!

He then turned around, offering his back without ever realizing he had not found the Devil Girl but instead mistakenly called out to Pandora, the girl Manpachi was supposed to meet.

Pandora :
What's this-sniff- you are offering to-sniff-give me a piggy back ride? That's really nice of you-sniff- I caught a cold.

Omori:
Wow you really have a stuffed up nose don't you? You should be careful of the breeze at night, you will catch a cold. You are leaving yourself open for disaster. You need to warm your body up from the inside.
And so on as he carried her.

Other notes:

The girl, Pandora, is probably supposed to be a prostitute. The clue to this is how she has her head cloth in her mouth. This was how Yotaka Soba 夜鷹蕎麦 (night-time Soba noodle sellers) advertised their wares. The "night-time Soba noodle sellers" began in Edo after the Great Meireki fire of 1657, where over 2/3 of the city burned to the ground. With a great demand for reconstruction and wages high laborers flooded the city. Since the majority of shops burned down, salespeople walked around calling out their wares on a pole. This was called Botefuri棒手振 and portable soba noodle shops were particularly numerous. The picture below by Utagawa Toyokuni 歌川豊国 shows a Kabuki actor named Matsugoro selling soba with a Botefuri shop on his shoulder.

Prostitutes that were masquerading as "night-time Soba noodle sellers" were referred to as "Night-hawk Soba noodle sellers." The origin of the term Yotaka 夜鷹 (Night-hawk) is based on the habits of hawks, which are active during the day and only sleep at night. Therefore these women "only sleep." As is shown in the illustration on the previous page, Yotaka are depicted biting their headcloth and carrying a rolled-up Goza 茣蓙 (a grass mat.) There are a few famous sayings about the Yotaka Soba noodle sellers.

夜たかそばねござの上へもりならべ

Night-hawk sellers spread their Soba on top of Goza grass mats

客二つつぶして夜鷹三つ食い

Two customers means a Night-hawk can eat three meals

The latter phrase refers to yet another name for Night-hawks, 二十四文 24 pennies. Two customers means the Night-hawk got 48 pennies. This phrase takes into account the fact that one meal of soba cost 16 pennies, so three meals a day would be $16 \times 3 = 48$.

Watanabe had purchased his gold charm from the temple and was strolling about. He had been taking his sweet time and suddenly, he realized with a shock, the sky was starting to brighten in the east.

Watanabe:
By the three treasures of the Buddha!
(Invoking the Buddha, the teachings of the Buddha and the monks that teach.) *It is nearly dawn. My body is liable to wake up soon! I need to get back before something terrible happens.*

Behind him the mischievous Shichihyoei Kagekiyo was also running late, and he had started to panic. Suddenly he saw the back of what he presumed was Mihonoya moving quickly past. He immediately grabbed the Shikoro of Watanabe's helmet and started pulling, presuming it was Mihonoya.

Watanabe, for his part, assumed the hand pulling his helmet belonged to the demon Ogata Ibaraki Doji and he did not have time to turn and check. He immediately began jockeying for position with what he assumed was his old adversary.

At this point the Scholar woke up at the inn and gave his back a good scratching and yawned two or three times.

Kagayikyo to Watanabe:

Hey, you aren't the Samurai I was looking for! What a blunder!

Watanabe:
If I only had eyes in the back of my head I could have figured it out! Looks like the body at the inn turned over and woke up! We made it back by the skin of our teeth! He was scratching his body so you and I have marks all over our faces, hands and feet. And I had just gone to the bath house last night and rid myself of fleas! Bad luck all around.

The demon Ibaraki Doji arrived late at Rashomon Gate. With Watanabe nowhere to be found the demon was left with nothing to grab hold of.

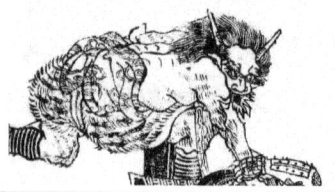

Ibaraki Doji didn't want to return to the body alone so he went to the meeting point at the entrance of the gate. Just then Mihonoya Shiro Kunitoshi came running up with his helmet on crooked, the Shikoro sticking up.
Ibaraki :

Hey! Who do you think you are? Stay out of the way! I was waiting here first!
And with that he grabbed the top of Mihonoya's helmet.

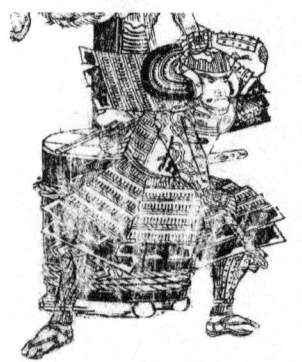

Mihonoya figured it was Kagehiko that was assaulting him.

Mihonoya :

No, no, no, not there. You are going to have to move your hand lower if you are trying to get a good grip on the Shikoro.

Hearing Mihonoya's voice Ibaraki suddenly looked at the face of the man he had grabbed. Realizing it wasn't Watanabe he shrieked like a crow. Then, they both jumped back into their tattooed bodies.

Meanwhile, Omori Hideshichi continued to carry Pandora on his back, thinking she was the Devil Girl. However, when he went to leap back into his tattooed body, Pandora was dropped and left stranded.

Pandora was mortified at having been stranded and became enraged. She started screaming her head off in anger, waking up Thunder, the bearer of the tattoo, and his wife. They tried to figure out what was going on, and even the landlord rushed in.

Pandora started screaming, *The man of this house abandoned me!*

Thunder protested, *I've never set eyes on this woman!*

However, with that accusation hanging in the air, his wife began to swell up with jealousy like a Mochi rice cake grilling on a stove. She exploded in a fit of rage and the couple began tearing into each other. During the fight, Thunder's Kimono came loose and dropped down, revealing the tattoo.

The landlord saw this and said, *Why, it's as if the devil woman has just fallen off his back! It's just the Samurai Omori there by himself!*

With that revelation everyone in the house was struck dumb.

	Pandora looked at the tattoo of Hideshichi and exclaimed, *I can't believe it! This is the guy who abandoned me!*
	Thunder's Wife: *Wait, you mean the tattoo…came out of his body?!"*
	Thunder: *Oh my, oh my!*
	Landlord : *Oh my land, oh my lord!*(a play on the word "landlord") And they continued in that fashion with all four talking at the same time. Landlord: *You are lucky half that tattoo fell off! Better check inside the sleeves of your Kimono, it might be in there.*

35

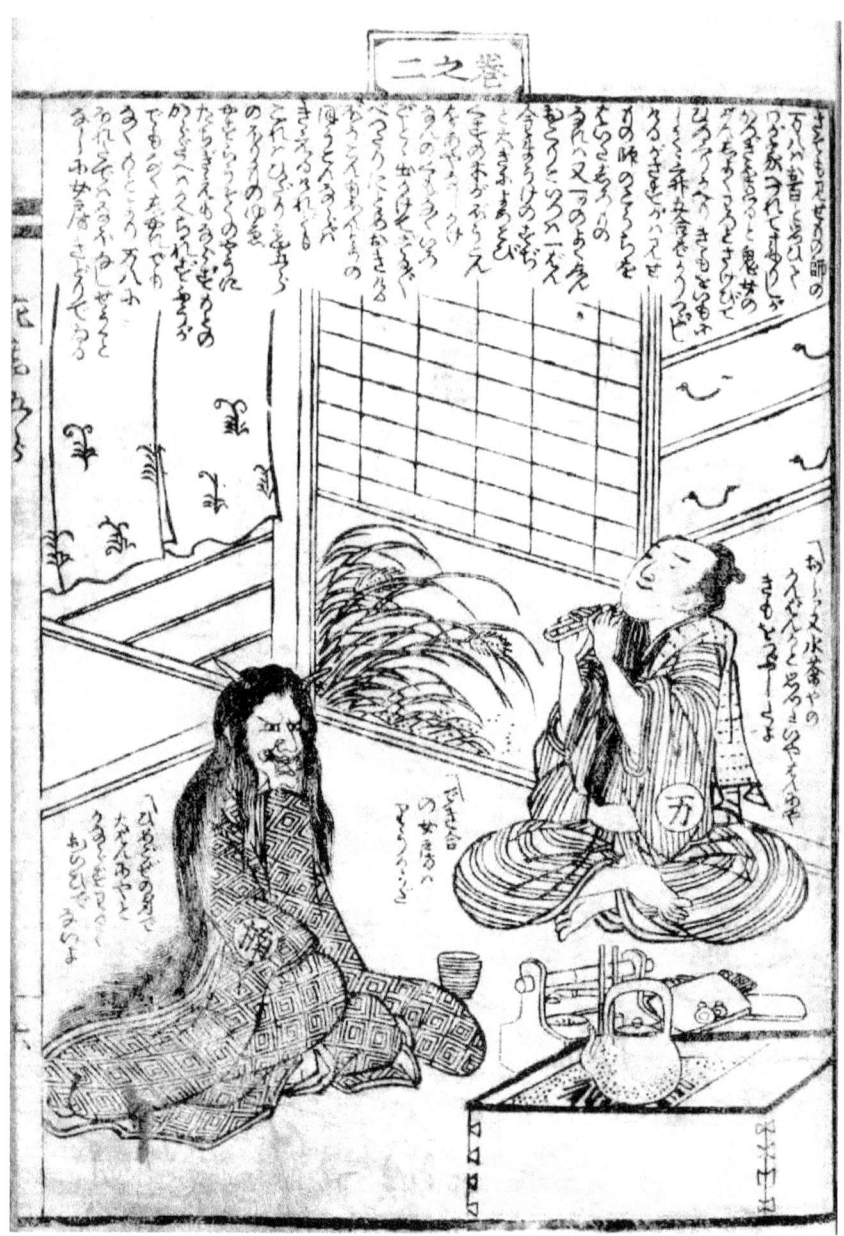

Meanwhile, the performer Manpachi had brought the girl he thought was Pandora back to his lodging. Pulling the scarf off her head, he was shocked to see the pale visage of the Devil Girl. He tumbled backwards like an overturned barrel of potatoes with shocked words rolling out of his mouth in an incoherent jumble.

However, being a seasoned performer, he quickly recovered from his fright as he was overtaken by another emotion, the lust for cash. Realizing her money making potential, joy spread across his face.

Then he began to manipulate the ghost of Kusunoki quite skillfully. He effortlessly wove a web of compliments that she was unable to untangle herself from.

If this apparition had been a real ghost, she would have been able to disappear, however she was a tattoo by the master engraver Lefty, therefore couldn't just disappear like a cheap candle.

Interestingly, while the Devil Girl was neither beautiful nor fashionable, something about her struck a chord with Manpachi. Or maybe his mind was just addled, but he began to think of her as his wife.

	Manpachi : *You know, I was thinking we could do a new show at the Tea Water House making you the lead performer. Good grief, that Hannya mask gave me a fright, I think you, my wife, have what it takes to make it big!*
	Devil Girl : *It won't matter if you dress me up like a princess, only evil comes out to this great Hannya mask.*
Note: This is the beginning of the second volume.	

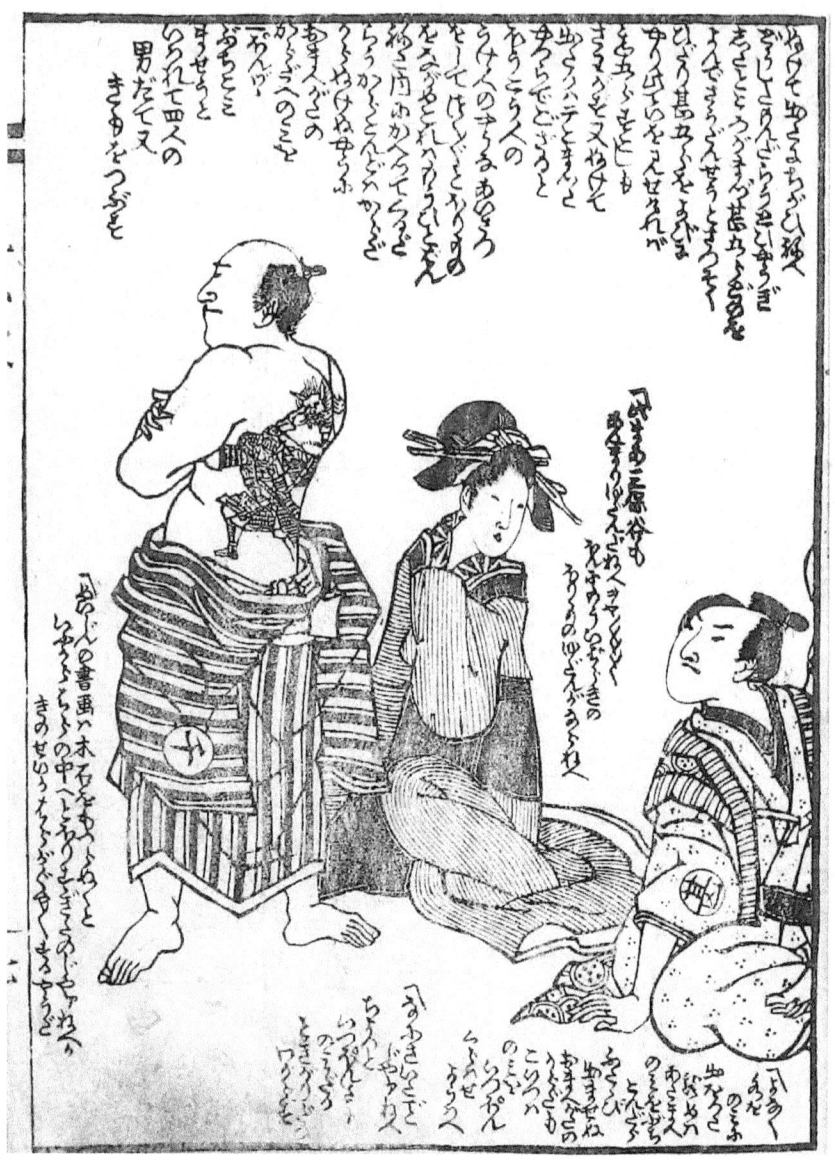

When Goose and Seal looked at each other's backs during morning tea they realized something was amiss. The engravings had switched bodies while they slept! The tattoo had Kagehiko grabbing the Shikoro of Watanabe's helmet instead of Mihonoya's.

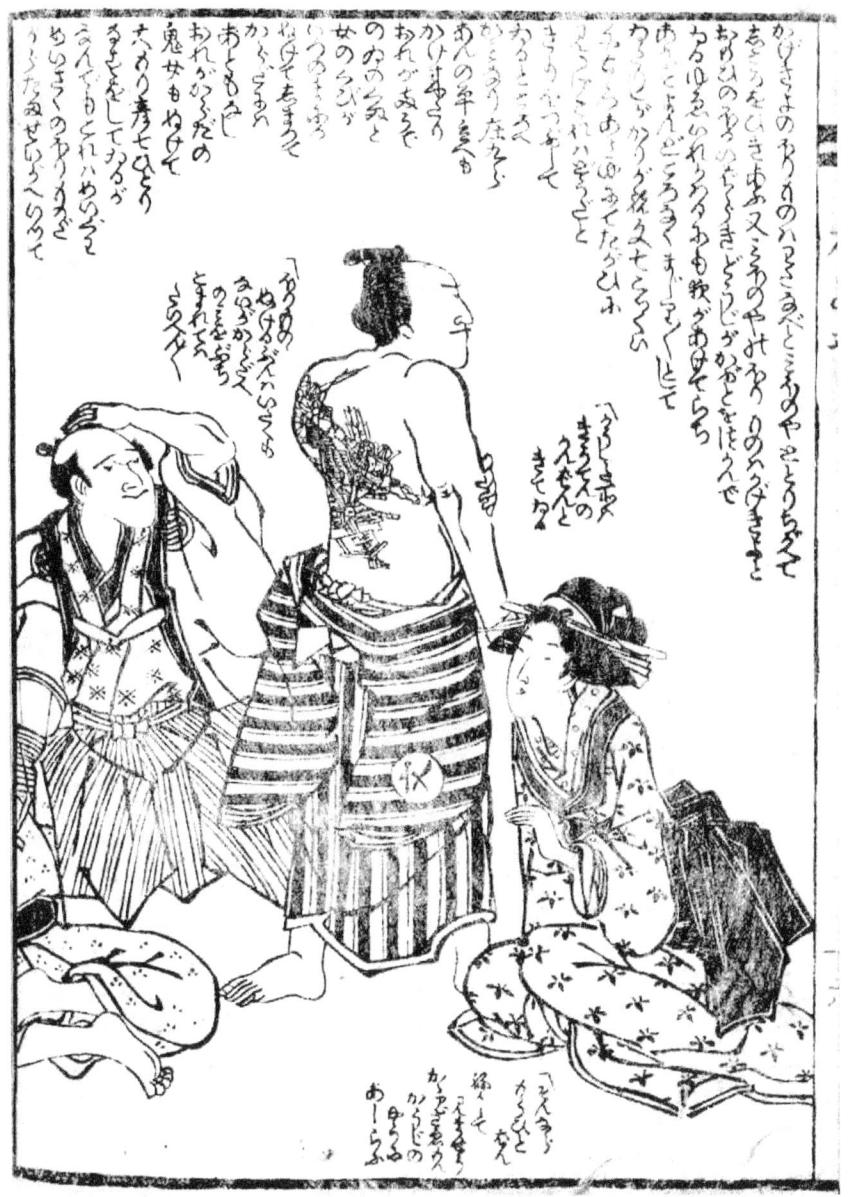

Further, Mihonoya's helmet was being grabbed not by the tattoo of Kagekiyo but rather by the tattoo demon Ibaraki Doji.

They were still in a state of utter bewilderment when Thunder and Safety came running up declaring, *The head of Inokuma and the woman have disappeared, there isn't a trace of them to be found! The Devil Girl disappeared from my body now it is just Omori Hideshiki all by himself!*

You know, we got a famous artist of create the designs and we had renowned engraver do the tattooing, it should be no surprise that they poured their souls into their work. Those should must have somehow pulled free. I've never heard of anything like this.

Goose:
I supposed we could get moxa treatments to burn off the tattoos?

Seal :
Nah, before we do that, let's sleep on it and see what the situation is in the morning.

Landlord:
Even though the tattoos flying off your body didn't hurt, getting a chisel pounded into your body would be quite painful, indeed.

Wife:
Looks like Sanponoya let his guard down again! Ha, ha, ha! You can't let your guard down even around the tattoo of the demon Ibaraki.

Seal:
They say a famous painter's work can pierce stone and wood. It may just be my imagination but I feel as if it's stabbed through my stomach. Maybe it's all in my head but something is going on down there.

The head of Inokuma and the woman with a scroll in her mouth stayed out so late they were unable to crawl back into their body.

They came to the somewhat questionable decision to continue their travels. There was even a Joruri play made about it.

Note: Joruri plays are performed with two people; a storyteller reading and another person playing the three stringed Shamisen. The Joruri plays were written in an even more indecipherable text, which has fortunately been transcribed, but are full of curious wordplay that is hard to translate. For example, it shifts from third to first-person, however I have tried to replicate it in English as best I can.

A Trip on Both Sides of the Road by Two Heads

Long ago in China there was the *Story of the Three Laughs*. A monk named Monk Eon had retired from the world and swore he would never cross the bridge over Tiger Gorge and thereby interrupt his seclusion. One day, two old friends came to visit his temple. At the conclusion of their visit he decided to see them off. The three old friends chatted amicably and before he knew it, the trio had stepped across the bridge. Their laughter shook the three of them more than it did the Kabuki actor Sakurada Jisuke Uko (this is probably some sort of jibe at the actor as he was still alive at the time.)

This off topic play will also interest the listener. This tale is destined to become legendary. Is this a love story though? As we roll through this story of two severed heads, lolling around as people sleep. It would be nice to think that though we held hands as we wandered around aimlessly, but we have neither hands nor feet.

Why are these two heads together? Did our bodies make a mistake? These details may seem a little dull but if we were to yawn the things we have stuffed in our mouths would fall out! Though your chest may get tight with tension like biting through the skin of a sweet snack all we can do is glare and roll our eyes about. Humorous and silly with a taste that is pleasing in the mouth.

Take the pipe out of my mouth and shove a piece of armor in it then roll this armless and legless form down a hill like a pumpkin. Once they get into motion on an endless hill there is no telling how far they may roll.

Inokuma:

Who on earth is going to read a bizarre Joruri play like this? If it is just following the story of two heads chatting as they go about it will end up like some erotic novel. Someone went to all the trouble to write a story that is easy to read but hard to understand.

The two heads went meandering along, lost as could be. They passed through the Awazabori neighborhood in Osaka and drifted into the Dotonbori entertainment area.

While resting there they heard that the Devil Girl ghost of Kusunoki who had taken up with the performer Manpachi, and was now his wife.

Thinking they would offer their congratulations, the two heads rolled over to Manpachi's family home, and into a whole new batch of trouble. At a stage in the Dotonbori section of Osaka a little acrobat by the name of Little Yellow Rose had a show. She was quite beautiful and a big hit. The heads rolled in with all the other customers for what was clearly going to be a sold out show.

Manpachi saw this show as his big chance. Yellow Rose was performing a scene from *The Tragic Love of Anchin and Kiyohime,* a story from the 10th century.

The Tragic Love of Anchin and Kiyohime, is about a man Anchin on a pilgrimage who stops for the night at a village. The daughter of the village mayor, Kiyohime, falls in love with him. The pilgrim departs, promising to return to visit the girl.

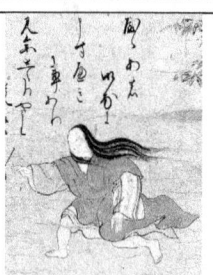

When Anchin does not return Kiyohime pursues him from temple to temple.

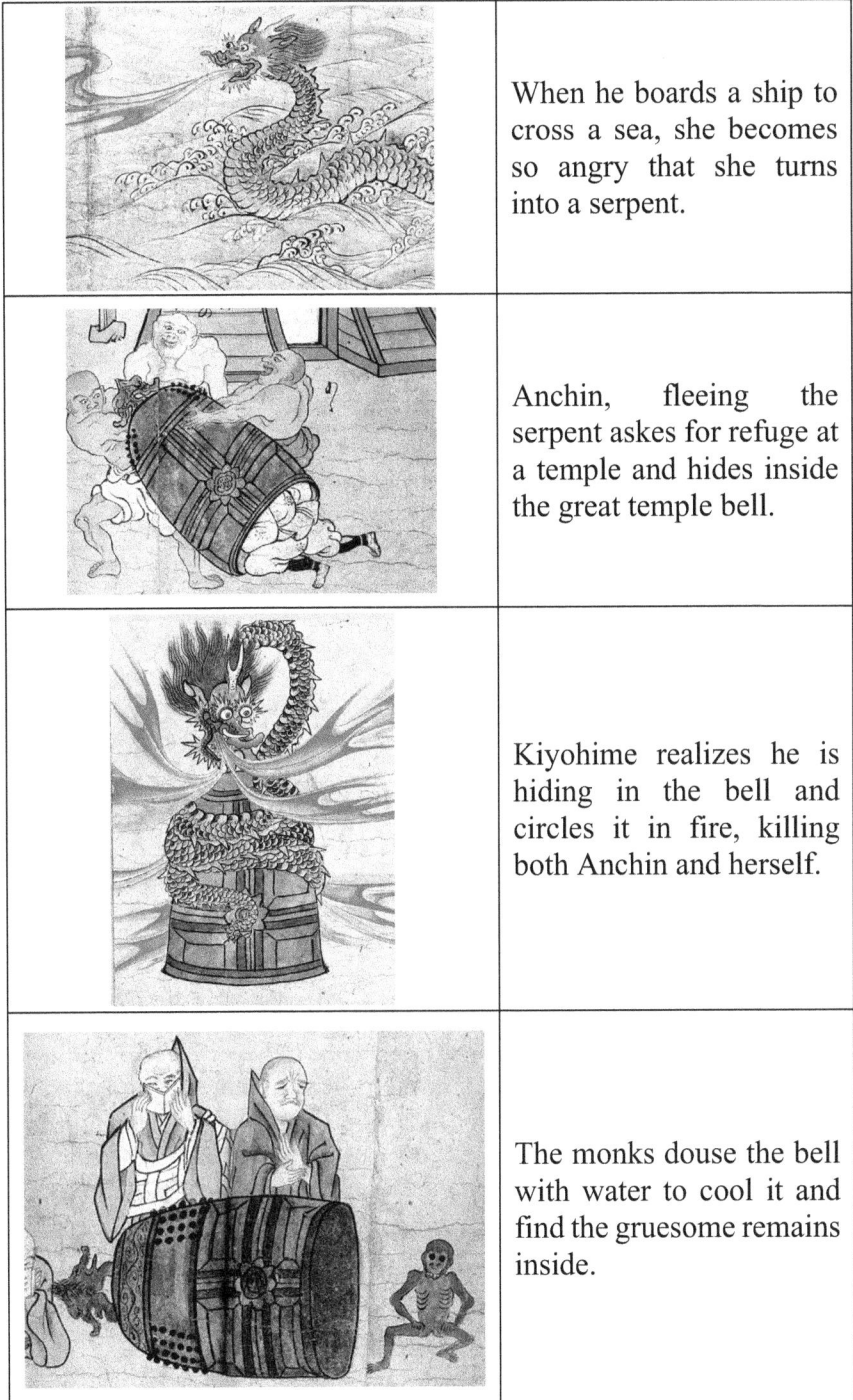

When he boards a ship to cross a sea, she becomes so angry that she turns into a serpent.

Anchin, fleeing the serpent askes for refuge at a temple and hides inside the great temple bell.

Kiyohime realizes he is hiding in the bell and circles it in fire, killing both Anchin and herself.

The monks douse the bell with water to cool it and find the gruesome remains inside.

For this scene Yellow Rose would climb inside the bell and emerge with a big acrobatic stunt. She would then return to the bell. Manpachi's plan was to have the Devil Girl emerge the second time and do acrobatics. A real Devil appearing will be a huge hit he had told the stage owner. Due to Manpachi's skillful persuasion the plan was agreed upon.

The spectators who had watched the first showing said,
Spectator 1: *The bell scene is fantastic! They could make 10 gold pieces a night with this act. Her acrobatics are top notch, probably best in Japan. She's the apple of her father's eye. She's a charming and a consummate professional, I suspect if we were to peel her she would be beautiful.*
Spectator 2: *She's so talented!*
Spectator 3: *She's beautiful!*
Spectator 4: *Wow! I wish I knew a girl like that!*

Priest:
She looks like a Shirabyōshi to me! (Shirabyōshi were female dancers, prominent in the Japanese Imperial Court, who performed traditional Japanese dances. They danced dressed as men.) But she certainly is beautiful!

Spectator 5: *She's beautiful and she is getting rave reviews! Way to go Yellow Rose!*
Spectator 6: *I praise you!*
Ticket seller (holding a wooden board with "tickets" written on it): *Who wants tickets to the next show?*

Finally, the it was time for Manpachi's plan to be put into action arrived. From out of the bell a real demon would emerge and it would be a rip roaring success.

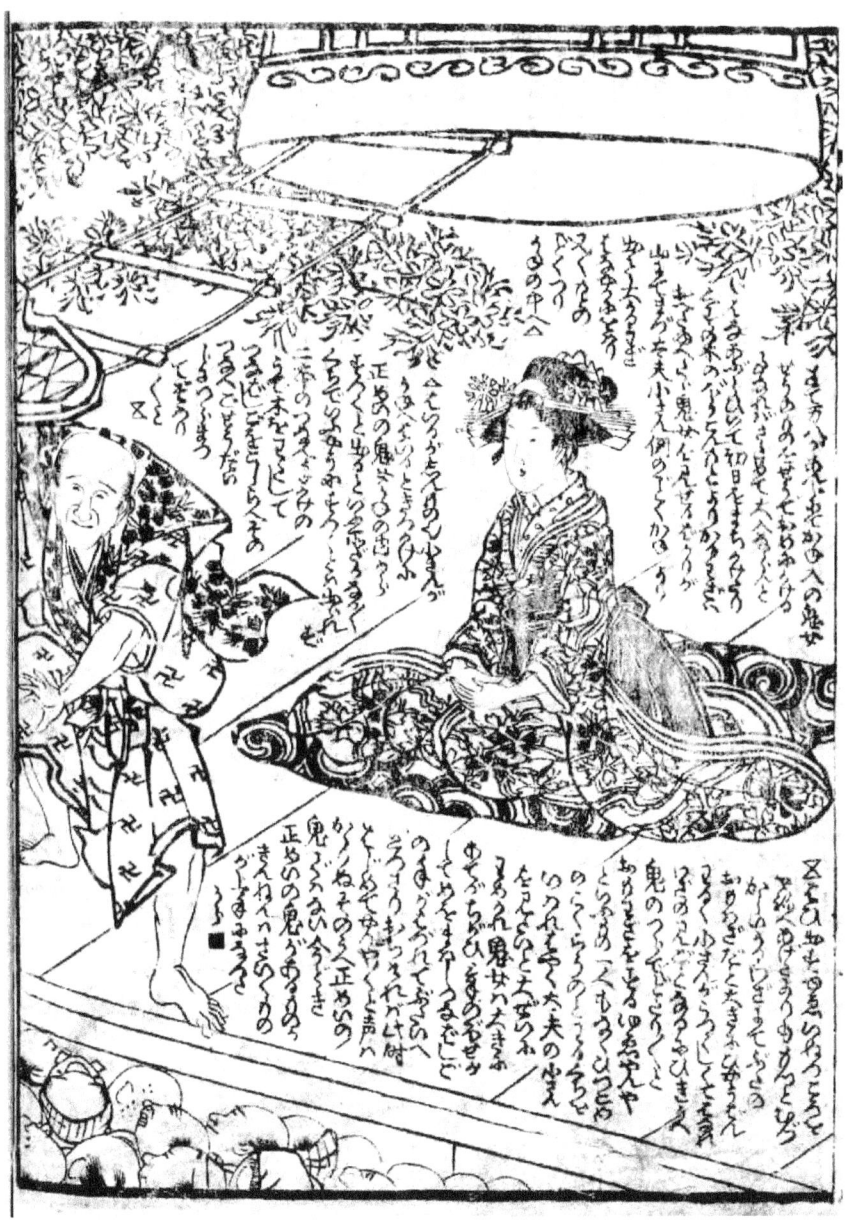

Unfortunately, the Ghost of Kusunoki was quite clumsy and completely unable to do any sort of acrobatics.

In the end all the audience saw was an awkward person dressed as a devil. Yellow Rose had emerged from the bell in a spectacular display of acrobatics. Having wowed the crowd she then re-entered the hanging bell. Then it was time for the new part. As soon as Yellow Rose entered the bell the real devil should emerge. And she did emerge…eventually.

How to put this… instead of nimbly traversing the rope ladder, the Devil Girl gripped it awkwardly as if her life depended on it. She slowly edged from one cross piece to the next, looking more like a dog trying to climb up the roof of a house. Far from making a light, acrobatic performance she showed the audience a heavy, lumbering scene that was received poorly.

When watching Yellow Rose the audience had been entranced by a beautiful performer executing difficult techniques with ease. When she turned into the girl with the devil mask on suddenly all deftness and ease left the performance. All that remained was a fumbling mess, and the audience responded with boos and calls for Yellow Rose to return. So the Devil Girl was something less than a big hit. But just at that moment she lost her grip on the rope ladder and crashed down onto the stage.

For the first time since she took the stage the boos from the audience stopped. They instead started yammering about whether or not the Devil Girl was really a devil because after all recently there were a lot of ways to fool people and so on and so forth. So the first day on the stage became her last day and all she had to thank for it was a bruised hip from the fall.

Devil Girl: *I suppose it could have been worse.*

The severed heads of Inokuma and the Woman were mixed in with the crowd and saw the whole thing. Though they were just heads they realized that they too needed to find some form of employment.

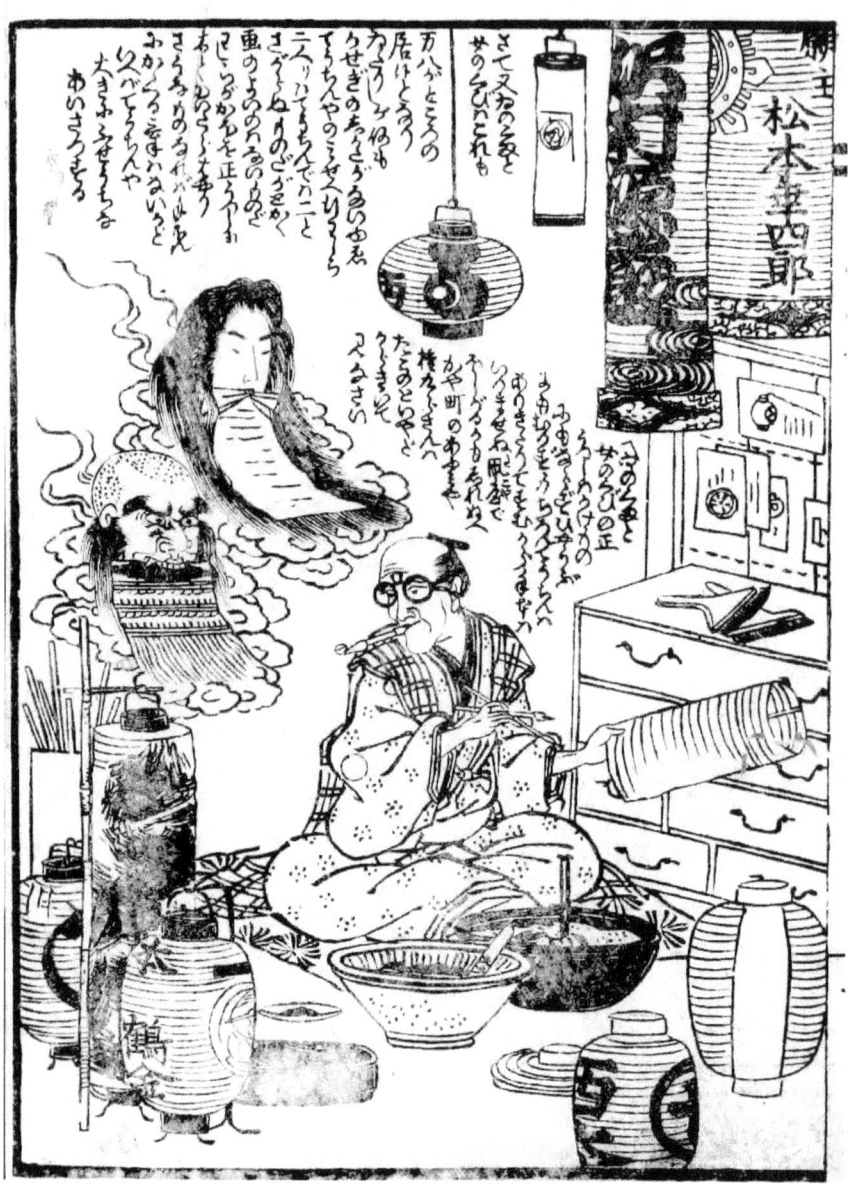

The heads of Inokuma and the Woman realized that they wouldn't be able to make a living working for Manpachi. They decided they had to find work so they first went to a lantern maker's shop.

Inokuma and the Severed Head of a Woman :

We were thinking making some lanterns based on us would be a good idea. If you drew our faces on a lantern they are sure to become popular. For starters maybe you should paint a couple of examples?

The lantern shop owner took one look at them and dismissed their proposal by saying,

Hmpf, I hardly think the severed heads of Inokuma and a Woman would be good subjects for a sign or even folding screens. Clearly no one would want a lantern with something like that on it. I won't even bother to try to paint a mock up. You could maybe try a kite shop. There is one just down the road.

Interestingly in a book called *Diary of Lord Fudo of Mikawa Island* by Santo Kyoden 1789 shows a pair of boys walking with just such a lantern. This may be a reference to that.

Manpachi had a daughter by the name of O-uso, Big Liar. She worked at a Samurai household, but she fell in love with a devilishly handsome boy named Yotaro.

Her emotional love eventually became physical love and caused a scandal in the household. Though they committed a crime and should therefore be executed, their Lord felt it would be a pity to kill two young people and wondered if there might be a way to find someone to take their place. Word of the Lord's willingness to find a solution reached Manpachi's ear and he was overjoyed at the news a chance to save his daughter's life. He was pouring all his concentration into the problem when heads of Inokuma and the Woman came in. He asked for their help in this matter and they quickly began preparations for the tattooed heads to take the place of his daughter and her lover.

Yotaro:

So we yell out Gyaaa and then fall backwards and immediately crawl under the curtain into the next room...that's the plan?

Inokuma :
If you want a good performance, after you cut the head off you need to throw it so it goes tumbling forward. I've got this dang piece of armor in my mouth so my teeth are going to hurt. Gah, they already ache now...

Note: This is the start of the third volume.

The execution began by calling the two forward onto the
Dodanba, the execution stage. The executioner drew his sword,
and the moment he raised it, the two lovers fell backwards.

In that instant the two heads were thrown forward, tumbling across the floor. Using this chance the two lovers crawled under the curtain to the adjoining room.

The two heads, one with a piece of armor in its mouth and the other with a scroll had severe expressions on their faces. The Samurai serving as the "executioner" did his best to conceal the faces of the heads with black cloth.

The two Samurai serving as inspectors had picked up hints regarding the Lord's wishes and were planning on glancing at the heads and then reporting the whole affair complete before returning to their rooms.

Samurai Inspector 1 :

Hmm, both heads have something in their mouths….and this may just be my eyes playing tricks on me, but with one cut of the sword this one seems to have been shaved bald! Quite a deft swordsman if he can cut a man's head off and trim his hair like a monk! Now that I look at him… it seems he still has long sideburns, very interesting!

Samurai Inspector 2 :

The lord said the woman's head should have a scroll in her mouth, but there is something strange about the other head….I may be mistaken but Yotaro was quite a handsome young man, but as you can see he has unruly hair all over his face and has his head shaved like a monk….ah, I think I understand! His living face and face in death are different!

After it was all was said and done, the response to the Devil Girl's performance was not all bad, so she was able to find work as a wedding performer.

Her role was to sweep away the evil in front of the wedding party. Typically a girl would paint a fearsome aspect on her face in order to frighten away evil. However, since she was born with the Hannya mask face she was ready to go at a moment's notice. Though she was hired she refused to ride in a palanquin. She had become quite taken with the notion of being carried around on someone's back. So one of the assistants in formal attire had to put her on his back. It looked like someone was carrying around the ferrywoman from the river Styx.

Onlooker 1:

I've been around a while but I've never seen the ferrywoman from the river of the dead wearing a formal Kimono. It's like New Year's Day and the Day of the Dead come all at once!

Onlooker 2:

I've seen people have their kitchens blessed by a temple priestess, and I get absolved of sins every June and December, but I can't say that I've ever seen someone in such a huge Hannya mask chase away devils.

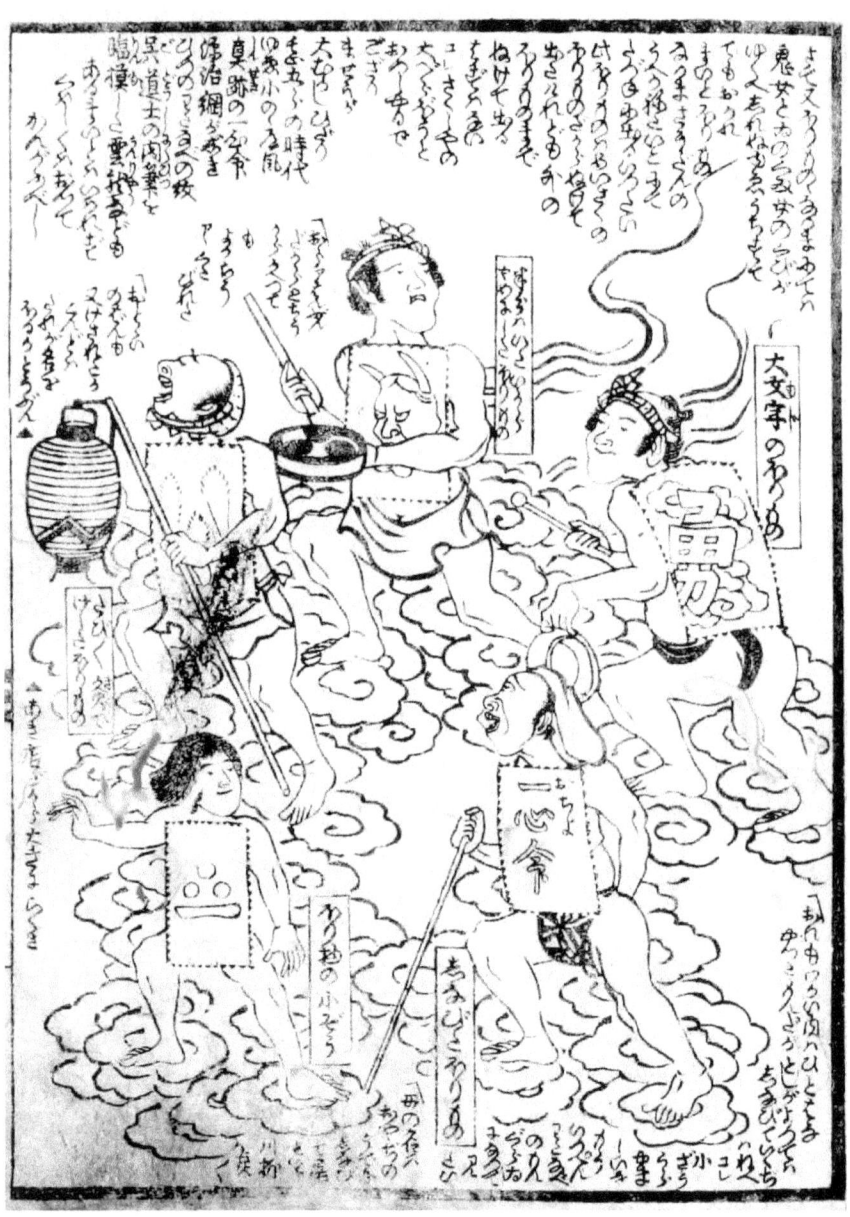

So then, there were several tattoos still missing from the group of tattoos. The Devil Girl as well as the heads of Inokuma and the Woman couldn't be found. It seemed likely they weren't planning on returning.

They speculated, *Well, we are all tattoos made by master craftsmen so it's possible for us to pull out of the body we were tattooed on, but we can't just go about like that forever…*

However, because this all happened long ago in Lefty Jingoro's era, they could call upon the tattoo of 一心命 Single Minded Purpose written by the great 9th century calligrapher Ono no Michikaze, the crest of the Watanabe household painted by Genchi Tsuna Watanabe himself, a dragon rising through clouds painted by a master calligrapher and others too many to name all gathered for the search.　For details, see the statements made by the men themselves:

Old Man With Withered Tattoo:

When I was young I was full of pride like a flower in spring, but now I'm a lot more cautious. I'm jealous of these youngsters like you, Little Fellow right there! Wish I could turn into that crest of the Watanabe family.

It hurts so I stopped halfway through my Hannya mask tattoo:

Hey, since I'm only half-done I will probably retire half-way through the search! Man I'm ready to lay down!

Little Fellow With the Crest of the Watanabe Family Tattoo:

I think you have my mother's name on your arm.

Note:
This refers to the tradition of tattooing the name of your lover on your arm.

Sometimes I Used Moxa to Erase part of my tattoo:

The other night I erased another name. Next time whose name should I tattoo I wonder? There is a lot of space left so no rush.

Note:
Moxa is short for moxibustion, a therapeutic treatment that was also used for burning off tattoos. Small pellets of dried leaves are lit on fire and placed on the skin. Source: Irezumi by Willem R. van Gulik 1982.

One Big Kanji Tattoo Guy:

No comment.

So the other tattoos went out banging a bell and pounding on a drum making inquiries.

Note:
The "One Big Kanji" is Yuki 勇 (bravery.)

So it was due to the efforts of the heads of Inokuma and the Woman that Big Liar and Yotaro were able to return safely to Manpachi's home. However, just as you forget how hot your tea is after you swallow it, so too did the lovers forget any sense of obligation to the two severed heads.

In fact they dismissed them outright, which angered the two heads, they said:
You are here because we were there, you don't have any say in the matter. You are stuck with us.

And with that the works carved by a famous engraver attached themselves to their hosts. The severed head of a Woman planted herself to the side of Big Liar's neck and Inokuma fixed himself to the side of Yotaro's head. Now each body had two heads. So the situation was like when Yamashiro Domain had two lords and two castles and a child was born. Byzantine plotting between men and women was sure to ensue. Manpachi and the Devil Girl were stunned at the situation

The left side of one body would be under the control of the tattoo while the other side was under the control of the person. Inokuma on the left would want to go to the bathhouse, while Yotaro would want to go out for lunch. The Woman's head on the left would want to go to the bathroom while the other side would want to fix her hair. Neither side could get along and their bickering only increased.

Inokuma and the woman took turns shouting, *Listen to me! You two stop badmouthing Manpachi! He is your father and your father-in-law. Such talk is inappropriate!*

71

Woman's head:
Hey, I'm getting hungry... why don't we have some tea and dried spiral cut cucumbers?

Yotaro:
Big Liar, I have something I want to tell you...

Big Liar:
I have something I want to tell you too...

Inokuma:
I have to pee...
Oops, I think I dribbled a little.

One day Big Liar and Yotaro got into an argument about
something or other. The two severed heads were right there for the
whole thing and got involved. This got the couple even more angry
and they started firing back.

Soon the heads of Inokuma, the Woman, Big Liar and Yotaro were started arguing and bickering in increasing intensity like a pounded rice cake swelling up on the grill. They started swatting and grabbing at each other just as Manpachi and the Devil Girl walked in. Soon there were six people grappling each other in a huge brawl.

At this point the other tattoos walked in. The manifestation of the Lord of Light Fudo as a dragon wreathed in clouds, the family crest of the Watanabe family, the Kanji Dedicated To One Purpose by the famous calligrapher Ono no Michikaze, Dedicated to Ochiyo (A famous Edo Era prostitute who serviced clients on a boat in Sumida River and even started a trend of such businesses), a tattoo of Kajiwara Sue (The 12th century Samurai who plucked the flowered branch of a plum tree and stuck it in his quiver), and a giant Kanji for "brave" along with many more famous tattoos from history. They took Manpachi aside and gave him detailed advice. The two severed heads were admonished and returned to the body they were engraved upon. With their task finished they returned from whence they came.

Inokuma: *I can't believe you! A woman that is nothing but a head with a scroll stuffed in her mouth and you are trying to charm Yotaro! Highly suspicious! There is no way that would work you are too fat and despite the fact that you are only a head you pretend to have arms! That is really annoying.*

The Severed Head of the Woman gave as good as she got:

What are you on about? Who do you think you are? If I'm just a woman with a scroll in her mouth, you are just a bald monk with a chunk of armor in his mouth. Can't you do any better than that? Even though you should be as patient as a monk you immediately get all misty eyed anytime you see Big Liar. It's so pathetic. You silly monk with your catfish whiskers and shoulder armor piece. You get me so mad! I hate you I hate you I hate you!

Big Liar :

There is nothing going on between me and my Inokuma! It's all in your head!

Yotaro :

*Why do you think there is something going on between me and the severed head of a woman...*After that Yotaro went on mumbling.

Manpachi :

You all never stop! What am I going to do with you all? You are like four pounded rice cakes getting stuck together while puffing up on the grill.

Devil Girl :

Sometimes I despair...

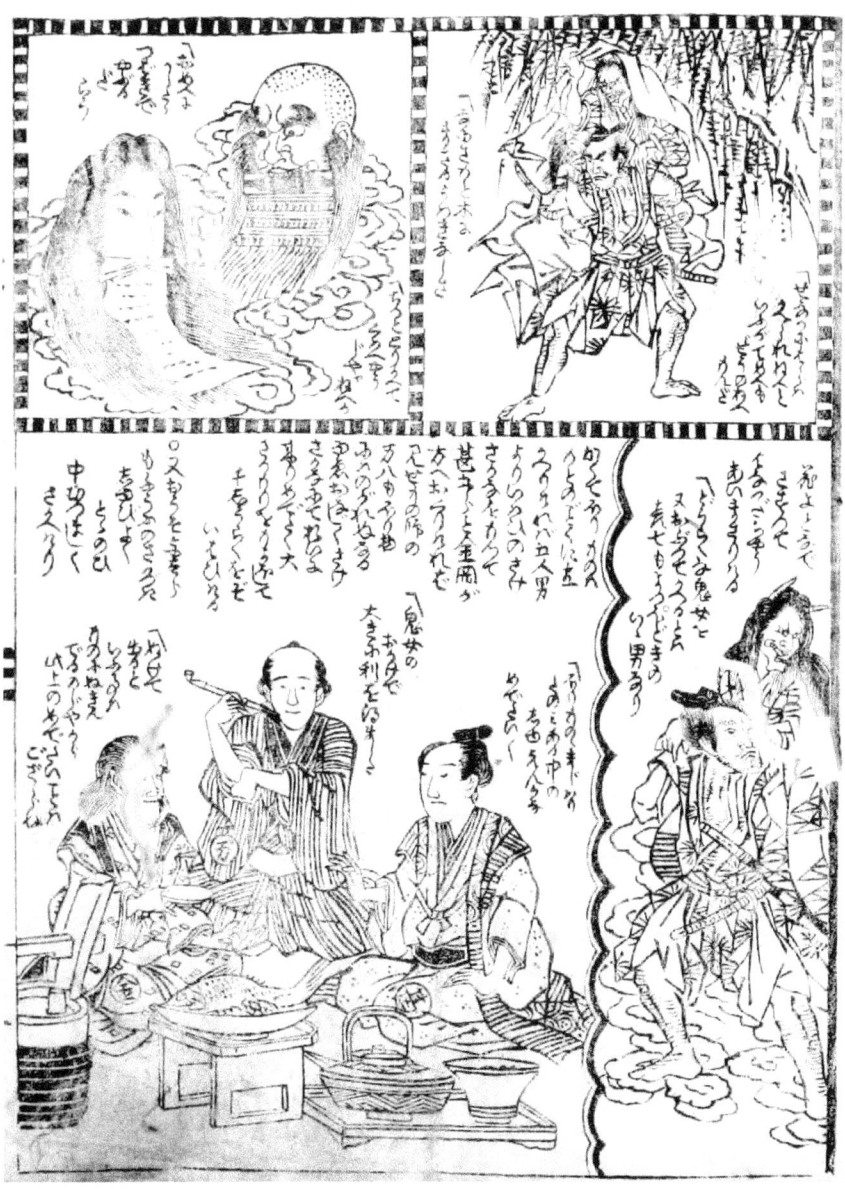

The group of tattoos including the dragon wreathed in clouds and Kajiwara Kagesue with his sprig of plum blossom had exhausted themselves admonishing the severed head tattoos but they had also convinced Omori to return.

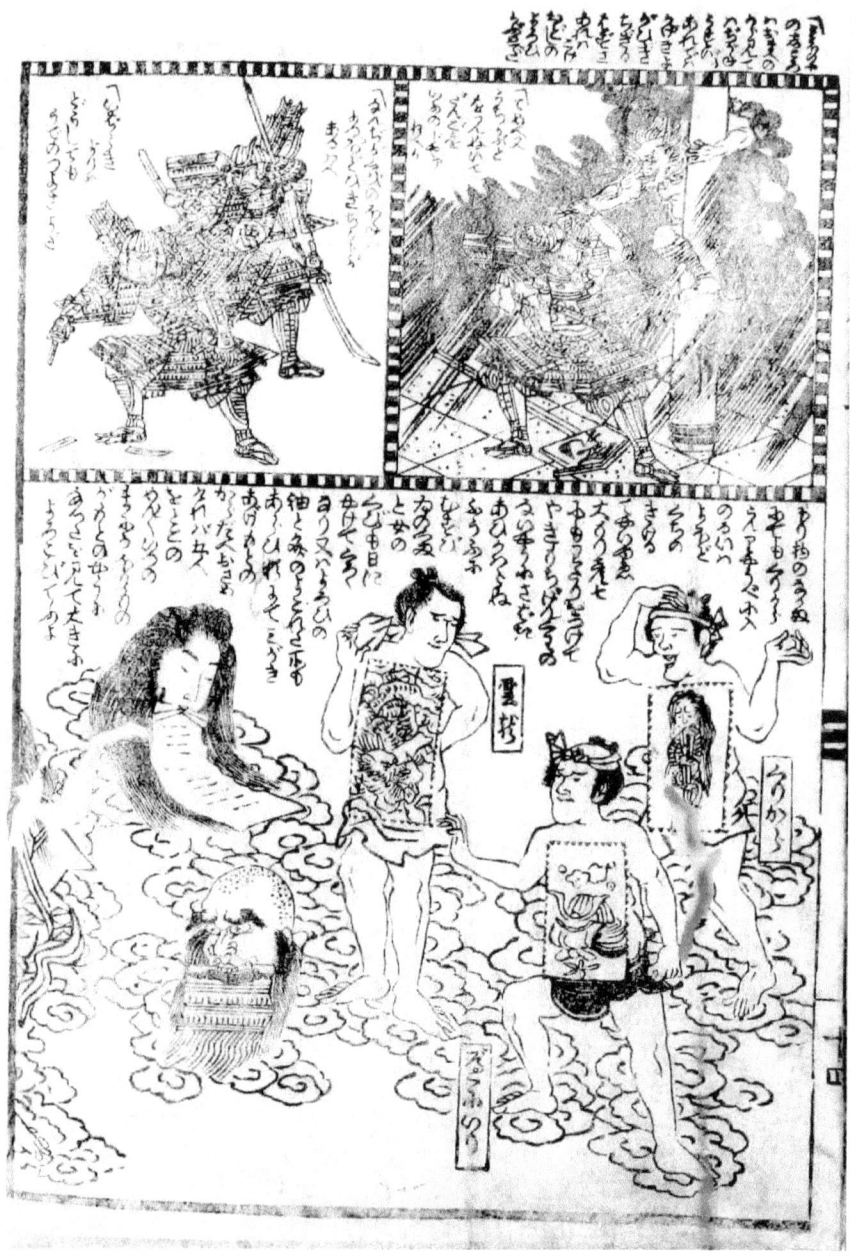

The various famous tattoos waded into the four way argument and somehow wrangled a truce. In the end the couples continued much as before.

Inokuma and the Woman had gotten sunburned badly over the course of their adventures. Both the piece of armor and the scroll were very dirty. The two heads and their accoutrements were bathed and scrubbed. When they had finished, and were newly cleaned and polished, they returned to their bodies.

When the five companions met again they realized that their tattoos had returned. At this revelation they were overjoyed.
The Devil Girl returned to her body and Hideshichi could hardly hide his joy as he carried her on his back.

Hideshichi :
Your stomach and my back haven't changed but you seem different.

Devil Girl:
Whatever do you mean? I haven't been cheating on you!

Inokuma :
You wouldn't be interested in trading items?

Severed Head of a Woman :
If we switched you would just drool all over it!

Ibaraki:
I think the workmanship on Mihonoya's helmet is not as good as yours, particularly the Shikoro flap at the back.
It's probably because Kagekiyo has been pulling on it.

Watanabe: *I don't think you know as much about armor as you think.*

Kagekiyo:
You've got a pretty strong neck!

Mihonoya:
I have to say Ibaraki's arm definitely has a stronger pull!

Note:
Left to right, Dragon in Clouds, Kajiwara Kagesue with a sprig of plum blossom and a severed head on a sword.

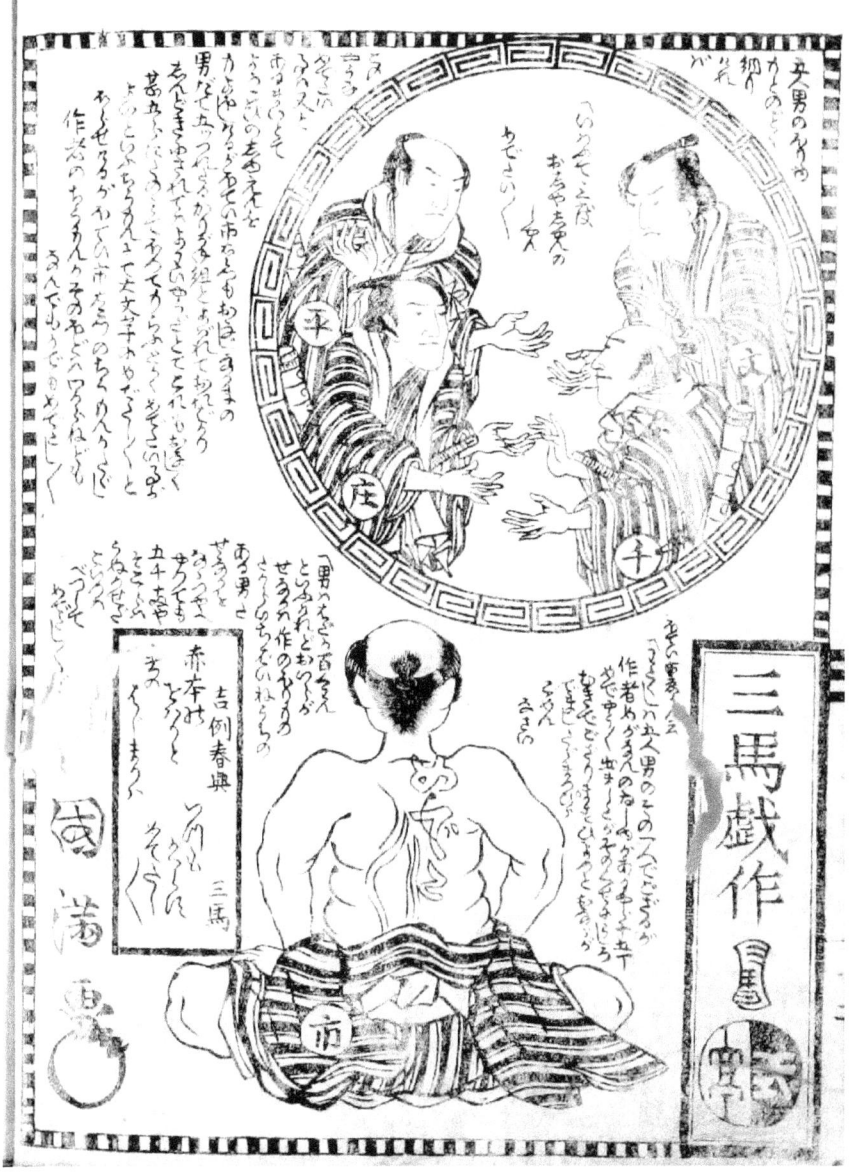

So all the tattoos returned from whence they came. The five companions decided to celebrate with a drinking party and they even extended an invitation to Lefty Jingoro and Kanaoka even Manpachi made an appearance, though mainly it was for the free Sake. The party capped off a the whole episode, and the group drank mightily.

Big Liar and Yotaro were wedded, tying off the ending to this story and congratulated them and wished for their harmonious future.

	Lefty: *Drinking with the tattoos that were once mixed up is a good celebration indeed!* Manpachi: *Thanks to the Devil Girl I made a lot of money!* Kanaoka: *Being able to pull out of something means you excel beyond that thing, truly a wonderful state of affairs.*
	The five companions, all assembled and enjoying good drink and company with their tattoos, returned to their proper places figured things couldn't get any better. However, Hotei Ichiuemon felt a little left out. I was the only one who lacked the courage to get a tattoo.
	So he decided to contact Lefty Jingoro and get an engraving on his body. He wanted it to celebrate the resolution of the last few days so it was *Everyone lived happily ever after* in large letters across his back.

It is not entirely clear if this is what Hotei Ichiuemon requested or it was the request of the writer of this tale but anyhow everyone lived happily ever after.

About the author:

式亭三馬
Shikitei Sanba 1776 - 1822

Shikitei Sanba was a writer who lived in the Edo Era. He was a writer of Kokkeibon 滑稽本 an illustrated tale with a witty and humorous story. The storys usually ended with a moral lesson. As a result of the Kansei 寛政 Reforms, which began in 1787, the content of *kusazoushi* changed from humorous material to instructional or edifying materials.

Sanba, whose name means three horses, worked at a book store from the age of 9 until he was 17. In 1794 at the age of 18 he began publishing his first work. Opened a book shop in the Nihonbashi area of Edo until it burned down in the great fire of 1806. After that disaster he moved and opened a pharmacy even finding success with his "Longevity potion of the mountain ascetic," and a "Edo Water," a kind of face cleanser. He later returned to writing and continued so until his death. His son, Little Three Horses 小三馬 continued both businesses after his father's death in 1822. A famous expression attributed to him goes,

Out there in the world, ghosts are not what I fear, idiots are what make me tremble

About the illustrator:

歌川国満
Utagawa Kunimitsu
?ー?

Utagawa Kunimitsu was an Ukiyoe "Floating World" illustrator in Edo. He was a student of Utagawa Toyokuni 歌川豊国 1769 - 1825. Toyokuni was very influential and made the Utagawa school the most famous woodblock print school in the 19th century.

Extra Material 1

The Ogre's Arm
By Hasegawa Takejirō 長谷川武次郎 (1853–1938)
Translated by Mrs. T.H. Kate James (?-?)

Hasegawa Takejiro published numerous illustrated Japanese Fairy Tales in English working with several different translators. This is a reproduction of 1889 edition.

THE OGRE'S ARM.

Long long ago, there dwelt in the mountain called Oyeyama a race of fierce ogres. The chief of these ogres was named Shutendoji, and he and his followers came down from time to time upon the city of Kyoto, causing great terror, and working much mischief. Entering in at the great gate called Rashomon, they robbed and killed all that came in their way, both men and women.

Now, in those days, there dwelt in Kyoto a brave warrior, named Minamoto-no-Raiko. This Raiko had four followers, the most daring of whom was named Tsuna. These followers were known far and near as Raiko's guard. In time of war they fought side by side, and in the intervals of peace they lived together in Raiko's castle.

It happened one dark and stormy night, during one of those brief intervals, that the four warriors were gathered round the charcoal fire, telling stories of war and adventure, and so wiling away the time as best they might.

"What dull times these are!" at last said Tsuna. "Is there no news, no hope of any fighting? I hate this quiet life!"

"News there is," answered another of the knights, who had just come into the room. "The ogres have begun their old tricks again.

"The ogres!" exclaimed the knights, in awe struck and terrified voices. But Tsuna laughed long and loud.

"Do you really believe such old wives' stories?" cried he. His companions made no reply, but shook their heads with sad and downcast looks.

At last, he who had brought the news looked up and said, "Tsuna, since you are so sure that there are no such creatures as ogres, will you go to the Rashomon to-night, and watch there alone?"

"Yes," answered Tsuna, "I

will go, and, if needs be alone, although I think one of you might bear me company."

But one and all protested that, though fair fight and honourable foe they feared not, yet the ogres they could not, and would not face.

Then up rose Tsuna, and at once began to prepare for his expedition. "How can we be sure that you really go to the Rashomon?" asked his companions. "What sign will you give us?"

"You know the notice-board which stands just outside the castle gate," replied Tsuna. "A new notice was posted upon it this very day. Well, if I carry the board, notice and all, and plant it down by the Rashomon where all may see it to-morrow morning, will that satisfy you, since my word of honour does not?"

They all cried out that this would satisfy them, and bade him good speed.

That very same night, mounting his horse, and taking the notice-board with him, Tsuna rode alone to the Rashomon, and there awaited the coming of the enemy, if enemy indeed there were.

Not a soul stirred abroad or passed through the gate-way, for all were in terror of the ogres. Furthermore the night was windy and rainy, and so dark that it was impossible to see a yard before you. Undaunted, the brave warrior kept his dread and lonely watch, and yet no creature came. The night was almost over, dawn was near, the storm had broken out afresh, when—A HAND, put forth from the roof of the gate-way, clutched Tsuna's head.

There, above him, stood an ogre of fearful aspect, his horrible head armed with a pair of copper coloured horns.

With his strong and bony hand he still grasped Tsuna's head and tried to lift him on to the roof·

Surprised and horror-stricken, Tsuna was fain to confess to himself that this must indeed be Shutendoji, whose very existence he had doubted. This was no time for thought, however, and Tsuna at once laid hold of the ogre and tried to pull him down.

Then a fierce struggle began. But Tsuna, being no match for the ogre in strength, would assuredly have been lifted from the ground, had he not succeeded in freeing one hand from the ogre's grasp. With this hand he drew his sword, and dealt one valiant blow at the ogre's arm. The arm fell, severed at the shoulder, and the ogre fled with a hideous yell. As all search for the monster was in vain, Tsuna at length took up the arm, and returned with it to Raiko's castle.

Next morning Tsuna, accompanied by his friends went to consult a famous wizard named Seimei as to what should be done with Shutendoji's arm. Seimei advised that it should be placed in a strong stone chest, and watched by Tsuna night and day, for seven days.

"But," said Seimei to Tsuna, "you must purify yourself by much fasting and prayer, and spend those seven days in holy contemplation, holding converse with none. Unless you faithfully carry out my directions, I foresee that misfor-

tune will surely follow."

Tsuna therefore caused a strong stone chest to be prepared, placed the ogre's arm within it, and, having purified himself by fasting and prayer, sat down alone to watch it. The doors were shut, and all visitors refused admittance. Alone, and wrapt in holy contemplation, Tsuna kept watch and ward.

One night, when the seven days and nights were almost accomplished, came a knocking at the gate.

" Who is there?" called out Tsuna.

"It is your old aunt from the country," answered a cracked and feeble voice. "Pray open the door."

Tsuna answered, "I am under a vow to hold converse with none, until seven days be past. I cannot open the door even to my aunt."

"I know that," returned the voice: But I have come a long way on purpose to see you. I am foot-sore and weary, surely you will not turn me away."

Tsuna still refused for some time; but at last he allowed himself to be persuaded to open the door.

"I have heard of your noble exploit," said the old woman as she came in, "and I have come all this long way to tell you how proud I am of my brave nephew."

"And where is the ogre's arm now?" she continued, when Tsuna had thanked her for her kindness in coming to see him.

"The arm is in this stone case," said he.

"Is it indeed now? Well, would you believe it?—although I have lived all these years, yet I have never in my life seen such a

thing.   Let me pray have one
little peep at it."

"I am sorry," answered Tsuna,
"but my vow forbids my opening
the case, or showing
the arm to

any one, even for a moment, until the seven days are past."

At this the old woman burst into bitter tears, refusing to be comforted.

Thereupon Tsuna, who was a soft-hearted young warrior, could withstand her no longer.

"Just one look then," said he, and lifted the lid of the chest.

The pretended aunt took up the arm, and seemed to be gazing at it in a kind of rapture, when, suddenly appearing in her true shape, which was none other than that of the ogre Shutendoji, she shouted, "My arm is my own again," and immediately vanished through a hole in the roof.

Tsuna, quickly recovering from

his surprise, rushed out; but not a trace of the ogre wsa to be found.

Sad and crest-fallen, the warrior bent his steps to the house of Raiko, and told him all that had happened. Raiko called his followers round him, and they there and then solemnly vowed that they would one day destroy the ogres in their stronghold of Oyeyama, or perish in the attempt.

Extra Material 2
Illustration of a demon attributed to Kose no Kanaoka 巨勢金岡

Engraving by Hidari Jingoro 左甚五郎 in the small shrine known as Akaiya 閼伽井屋 at Mii Temple 三井寺 in Shiga Prefecture.